*For Rocky Lawson,
the first pirate I ever met*

First published 1994 by Walker Books Ltd
87 Vauxhall Walk, London SE11 5HJ

This edition published 2005

© 1994, 2001 Colin McNaughton

The right of Colin McNaughton to be identified as author
of this work has been asserted by him in accordance with
the Copyright, Designs and Patents Act 1988

This book has been typeset in Plantin

Printed and bound in Great Britain by J.H. Haynes & Co. Ltd

British Library Cataloguing in Publication Data:
a catalogue record for this book is available from the British Library

ISBN 1-84428-138-8

www.walkerbooks.co.uk

CAPTAIN ABDUL'S PIRATE SCHOOL

COLIN McNAUGHTON

WALKER BOOKS
AND SUBSIDIARIES
LONDON · BOSTON · SYDNEY · AUCKLAND

Dear Diary,

Well, here I stinking am!

My first stinking day at Captain Abdul's Pirate School. My stinking dad has sent me here because he says I'm a big softie! (Just because I like writing poems and painting pictures!) He says it will toughen me up. He says a kid my age should jump at the chance of becoming a pirate. He says that when he was a kid he wanted to be a pirate and so should I.

He says I should be grateful.

Well, I say, "Nuts!" and I say, "Steaming cowdung!" and I say, "I hope he swallows his pipe!"

P.S. I have a secret.

I have smuggled my little dog Spud in my trunk. He's the only friend I've got in the whole stinking world!

We were met at the door by Captain
Abdul himself: hairy, scary and with more
bits missing than a second-hand jigsaw.

"Follow me upstairs, me little buccaneers,"
said Captain Abdul, "an' we'll get yer
kit stowed away, oooh-arrgh, that we will.
Ha-har, oooh-arrgh!"

to meet the other teachers...

Next we were given our school
uniforms and told to introduce ourselves.

Jim
Silver

Françoise
du Plonk

Ching Yih

Ali
Khoja

16

Unfortunately, Spud thought
this included him! Luckily the captain
likes dogs and said he could stay
(for a small fee).

Pickles

Henry
Morgan

Rosemary
Lavender

Woof!

Spud

I was a bit nervous about meeting the other kids but they don't seem too bad – they look just as miserable as me.

Tom Tew

Anne Bonney

Frankie Drake

Samuel P. Chop

We then had supper and went to bed,
where I wrote this and cried a bit for
my mum.

Simon
Smee

Ben
Gunn

Jack
Rackham

Beryl
Flynn

Mary Read

Bartholomew
Sharp

Dear Diary,

Woke up this morning and stood up in bed. Forgot I was in a hammock – bit of a headache. I was brushing my teeth when Bully-boy McCoy came in.

"What yer doin' that for?" he asked.

"If I don't, sir, my teeth will go black and fall out," I replied.

"What's wrong with that?" he said. "Who ever heard of a pirate with nice teeth!" And he confiscated my toothbrush!

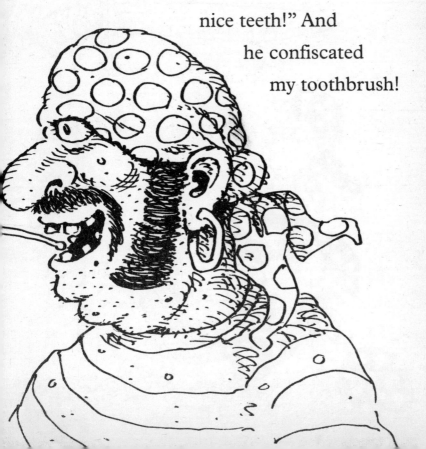

Today we studied history. Portobello Billy told us an exciting story about Calico Jack the pirate, set in his favourite place – the West Indies.

Dear Diary,

We were queueing for breakfast this morning when Walker the Plank came over and asked Rosemary Lavender if she was pushing in.

"Yes, sir," admitted Rosemary.

"Well done!" said Walker the Plank and walked away.

Today's lessons were maths and geography. In maths we learned about angles. (You use them when aiming cannon.) In geography we learned where the West Indies are and how to read treasure maps.

Dear Diary,

The beastly Captain
Abdul has scolded me
for being too neat
and tidy. He suspects
me of brushing my hair –

"Combs an' hairbrushes,
the possession of,
is a floggin' offence,
oooh-arrgh!" he told me.

Today we had arts and crafts.
We learned how to make cannon balls,
swords, fake money and how to put
model ships into rum bottles.
(Spanish Omar Lette very kindly
emptied the bottles for us.)

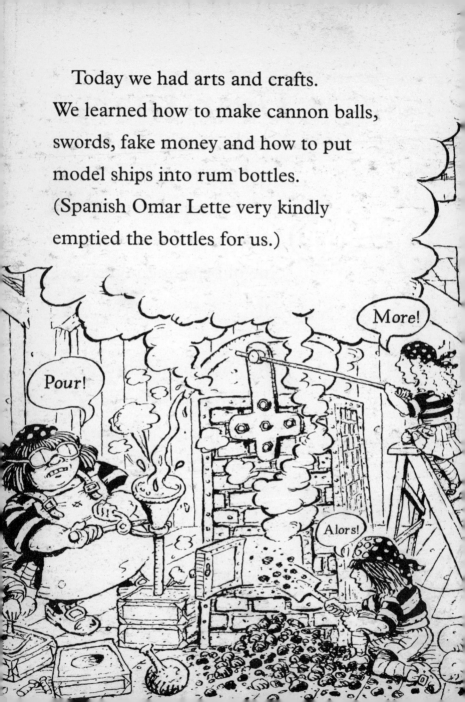

Dear Diary,

Last night we were doing our homework when Riff-raff Rafferty came in and caught little Simon Smee copying from another boy.

"Was you cheatin', boy?" howled Riff-raff.

"Yes, sir," said Simon Smee in a small voice.

"Good boy!" yelled the teacher. "Go to the top of the class!"

Today we learned how to speak
pirate. Can't wait till next week's lesson.
It's pirate swearwords!
Oooh-arrgh!

Dear Diary,

The teachers had a party last night! They kept coming up and saying it was much too early to be in bed and why weren't we having a midnight feast or rampaging round the town looking for trouble!

"Why, when I was your age," said the captain, "I already had a wooden leg! Oooh-arrgh!"

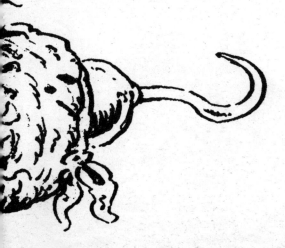

When the captain finally woke up today he bellowed, "Fresh air is what we need, oooh-arrgh! We're goin' to sea!"

For the rest of the day we sailed around the harbour in the *Golden Behind*, learning pirate stuff.

Wheeee!

Dear Diary,

Tricked! Betrayed! Duped! Fiddled! Fooled and double-crossed! Last night, after I'd taken Spud for a walk, he ran into the staffroom and I followed him in.

From the shadow of the captain's hammock, hidden by clouds of tobacco smoke, I heard terrible things…

"KIDNAP!" I yelled, when I got
back to our quarters. "Captain Abdul
and his dirty double-crossing teachers
are going to kidnap us tonight and when
our mums and dads arrive tomorrow for
parents' day, all they will find will be a
ransom note! We must do something!"

Arrgh!

"But what?" asked
the kids.

"MUTINY!" said I.
"We get them before
they get us!"

"YES!" everyone
shouted.

"Shush!" I hissed.
"Get your swords
and follow me. Tom,
you bring the ropes."

"Aye-aye, Captain!"
said Tom. "I mean,
yes, Pickles."

46

Armed to the teeth with swords
and ropes, our fearless band of pirate
pupils crept down to the staffroom.

I gave the order
and we attacked!
The battle was over in minutes.

49

We swarmed all over the pirate teachers
and tied them up with so much rope they
looked like cocoons!

We rolled the teachers out onto
the quayside.

One of the kids shouted, "What now?"

"We sail for the West Indies!" I cried.
"Who's with me? Who really wants to
be a pirate?"

"ME! ME! ME!" they all shouted.

"Good!" said I. "Raid the kitchen, fill
the water barrels and get the ship ready.
We sail in ten minutes!"

I wrote a note to our parents telling
them what had happened,
pinned it to Captain
Abdul and we set sail.

Dear Diary,

(six months later)

This is the life!

We now call ourselves "Pirate pirates" because we only steal from other pirates.

On our last raid we found out that pirates from all around the world had heard about our mutiny.

Thinking how well taught we must
have been, they have sent their kids to
Captain Abdul's school! Abdul claims
the mutiny was all his idea – part of his
teaching plan. The scoundrel!

And so everybody is happy: Captain
Abdul because his school is a roaring
success and our parents because we
send lots of treasure home.

The kids are happy because they get to sail and swim and fight and fire cannon and rob bullies and stay up all night!

And me? Well, I paint my
pictures and write my poems and
I'm captain of my own pirate ship!
Who could ask for anything more...

I'm Captain Maisy Pickles –
the happiest girl in the whole,
wide, wonderful world!

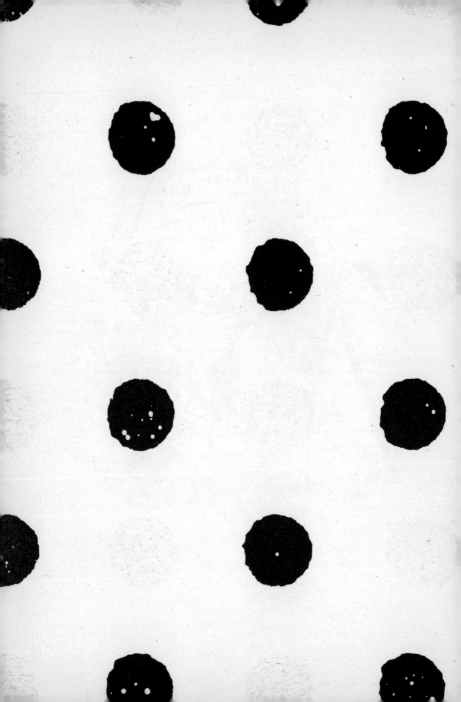

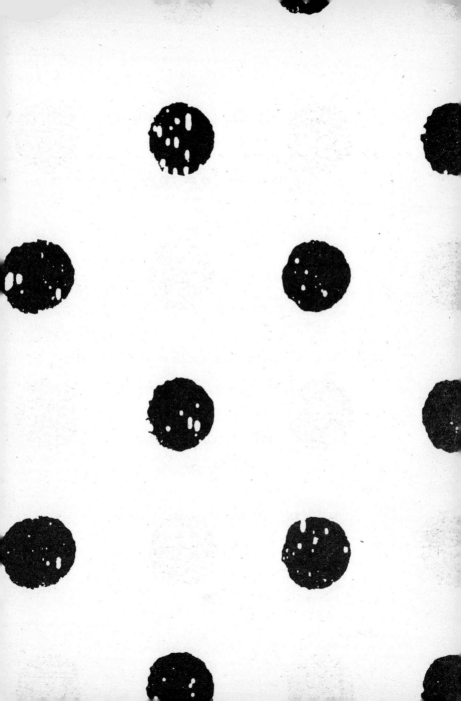

Books by the same author:

I'm Talking Big!

Jolly Roger

Making Friends with Frankenstein

There's an Awful Lot of Weirdos in Our Neighbourhood

Who's Been Sleeping in My Porridge?

Wish You Were Here (And I Wasn't)

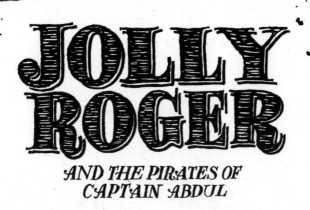

JOLLY ROGER

AND THE PIRATES OF CAPTAIN ABDUL

Avast, me hearties!
Climb aboard the *Golden Behind*
for the timber-shivering adventures
of miserable landlubber Roger –
and the smelliest, hairiest, scariest
bunch of pirates you ever did see!

"Energetic romp
of a story ... plenty of jokes."
The Sunday Times